Enid Blyton ™

In The King's Shoes

Illustrated by Pam Storey

Once upon a time the brownie pedlar Twiddles was sitting down by the lane-side mending a kettle. As he sat there, who should come along but the King of Brownie Land himself! He was walking slowly, as if he were tired. He saw Twiddles sitting by the lane-side and he sat down by him.

"Your Majesty, can I run to the nearest cottage and get a chair for you?" said Twiddles, jumping up and bowing.

2

"No," said the King. "Let me sit in the grass for once if I wish to. My shoes hurt me. I shall take them off for a few minutes while I talk to you."

The King slipped off his beautiful, highly polished shoes with their silver laces.

"My word!" said Twiddles the pedlar. "I'd dearly love to be in your shoes for a little while, Your Majesty."

"You would, would you?" said the King. "Well, it's a silly, foolish wish of yours, but I'll grant it! Get into my shoes – and you'll find yourself King! I'll be a pedlar for a few hours!"

Hardly believing his ears, Twiddles got into the King's shoes. They fitted him perfectly. He stood up and gazed down at himself in astonishment. He was dressed like a king – and the King was dressed like a pedlar! Such was the magic in the King's shoes! Whoever wore them could be the King himself!

"Go down the lane and you'll meet my servants," said the King. "Good luck to you! I'm going to have a snooze in the shade here and listen to the birds singing."

Twiddles went down the lane, holding his head high and looking as proud as could be. He was King! King! How grand it felt!

He saw some men hurrying towards him.

"Your Majesty, Your Majesty!" they cried. "You will be late for the opening of that sale of work. Hurry, Sire!"

"Dear me," thought Twiddles, "so I am to open a sale of work and everyone will bow to me and cheer me. How fine!"

He hurried to a waiting carriage and climbed into it. He drove off quickly to the next town. How the people there cheered him! He opened the sale of work and read a speech that was put before him. He stood in the hot sun for about an hour, shaking hands with all kinds of brownies. He began to feel tired.

"I say, isn't it about time for dinner?" he asked a courtier nearby.

"Not nearly," said the brownie, looking surprised. "You have to review your troops of Scouts next, Your Majesty. Have you forgotten?"

"Oh well," thought Twiddles. "It will be fun to ask the Scouts all about their camp fires and the best way to boil kettles on them. I am sure I could teach them a thing or two about that!"

But to his surprise, when he began to talk to the Scouts about this sort of thing his courtiers nudged his arm and frowned.

"Your Majesty is not supposed to know how kettles are boiled or camp fires are made!" they whispered. "Those are not the things a king is interested in."

"Dear me!" thought Twiddles. "How dull it must be to be a king all one's life! How hungry I am getting! Whenever are we going to have dinner? I guess it will be a fine one, with lots of marvellous things to eat and drink!"

But, to his great disgust, as soon as he had quite finished with the Scouts he was hustled into his carriage and driven off to see a new ship being launched – and a footman presented him with a little packet of sandwiches to eat!

"Is this all my dinner?" asked poor Twiddles. "Just sardine sandwiches? Well, well, well! I'd be better off if I were a pedlar! I'd at least fry myself

bacon and eggs, with an apple or two to follow!"

"Your Majesty, there is no time for you to have a proper lunch today," said the courtier who was with him. "You have to be at the dockyards in half an hour. And after that you have to visit a hospital. And then there is the flower show to go to."

"Do you mean to say that all these things are on one day?" asked Twiddles in disgust. "Don't I get any time off at all?"

"Your Majesty is acting very strangely today," said the courtier, looking troubled. "You promised to do all these things – and a king must keep his promise."

Twiddles launched the new ship. He rushed off to the hospital and walked around the wards and spoke to everyone in the beds there. By the time he had finished, his feet felt as if they could not walk another step and his face was stiff with smiling so much. He badly wanted a cup of tea.

But no! He had to go to the flower show next and miss out his tea altogether! He was very hungry as he had only had sandwiches for dinner.

He yawned and yawned at the flower show and his courtiers looked most disgusted with him. He didn't at all want to see the beautiful flowers they showed him. He didn't want to smell any of them. He just wanted to sit down on a chair and have a cup of tea all by himself.

When the flower show was over he was driven to the palace. Twiddles was thrilled to see it shining in the evening sun. The people cheered him as he passed. Twiddles forgot about his dull day and waved his hat to the people. But that was not the thing to do at all. He had to bow stiffly from left to right and from right to left. He got out of the carriage and went up the long flight of steps.

"I want a jolly good meal now," he said to the courtiers.

They looked surprised. "Your Majesty, you will only just have time to change into your best uniform and get ready for the big military dinner tonight," they said.

"Oh, well," thought Twiddles. "I shall certainly have something to eat at the dinner – and I shall look handsome in a uniform, too."

The uniform was tight and stiff. It cut him round the legs. It cut him across the shoulders. It was heavy. But still, he did look very handsome indeed. He went down to the dinner.

But before he could sit down he found he had to shake hands with two hundred guests! Twiddles was not used to shaking hands with so many people and his hand soon ached terribly. At last he sat down to the table.

He had a famous general on one side and a famous prince on the other. They both talked so much that Twiddles hardly had time to eat anything, because he had to keep saying, "Yes, certainly," and, "No, of course not!" almost every moment.

The dinner took a long, long time. Twiddles got very bored. He thought the general and the prince were both very silly. He wished they would stop talking for just one minute. But they didn't.

At last bedtime came. Twiddles felt as if he was being squeezed to death in his tight uniform. He could hardly breathe. He was so very, very glad to get out of it. His servants left him when he was ready for bed. He stood and looked at the beautiful bed ready for him – and he shook his head.

"No," said Twiddles. "I don't want to sleep in you – and wake up in the morning to rush about all day long doing things I don't want to do. It's a difficult thing to be a king. I'd rather be a pedlar. I'm free, but a king is not. A king has many masters and must do as he is told all day long – a pedlar has no master and is free as the air! I'm going back to be a pedlar again!"

He slipped out of the palace in his sleeping-suit. He made his way to the stables. He jumped on a horse and rode bareback to the lane-side where he had left the King.

There was a small light there – the remains of a camp fire. A man was sleeping peacefully beside it. It was the real King!

Twiddles woke him. "Wake up!" he said. "I've come back. I'm not a good king! I got hungry and bored. I'd rather be a pedlar."

The King sat up and stared at him.

"Well, I got hungry and bored, too, when I was a king," he said. "I like being a pedlar. It's lovely! Just do what you like and nobody to say, 'It's

your duty to do this or that!' No, Twiddles, you go on being a king. I don't want to go back!"

Twiddles kicked off the King's shoes. He had put them on to come back in. In a trice he had changed once again to the untidy pedlar he had been that morning. Even his beautiful sleeping-suit disappeared and he was dressed in his same old clothes. But the King was dressed in the fine sleeping-suit – he was no longer the pedlar!

The King got up. "Well, well," he said, "I suppose I had better go back. After all, it's my job. I must do it as well as I can for the sake of my people, who love me. But oh, Pedlar, you can't think how I have enjoyed today!"

"Yes, I can," said Twiddles, patting the King kindly on the back. "You've enjoyed today just as much as I shall enjoy tomorrow. Now, goodnight, Your Majesty, and pleasant dreams!"

Twiddles lay down by the fire. The King galloped back to the palace on the horse. And when the pedlar awoke next morning he wasn't at all sure that it was nothing but a dream!

"Poor old King!" he said. "He has the hardest job in the world. Won't I cheer him when I next see him! But I wouldn't be in his shoes for anything!"